# Murf the Monster

by NORA LOGAN

illustrated by Mort Gerberg

## SCHOLASTIC INC.

NEW YORK • TORONTO • LONDON • AUCKLAND • SYDNEY

ISBN 0-590-33290-2

12 11 10 9 8 7 6 5 4 3 2 1          7          5 6 7 8 9/8 0/9

Printed in the U. S. A.                                    11

This book is for Roger.

# Scholastic Books in the Pick-A-Path Series
## How many have you read?

## READ THIS FIRST

Are you ready for some really fantastic adventures?

Start reading on **page 1** and keep going until you have to make a choice. Then decide what you want to do and turn to that page.

Keep going until you reach **THE END.** Then, you can go back and start again. Every path leads to a new story!

It is all up to you!

It's eleven o'clock on a summer night.
As a special treat, you and your brother
Jake are staying up late to watch a
meteor shower. You're sitting on Death
Rock, which juts out over Murphy's
Creek. It is the highest spot for miles
around.

The night is very dark and quiet.
You can't help feeling a little scared.

Suddenly the whole sky lights up
with flashing meteors. Then one streak
of light separates from the rest. It gets
closer and closer. It's so bright you
have to close your eyes.

A moment later you hear a loud
splash in the water below you. "A meteor!" you shout. "Or maybe even a
flying saucer!"

*Turn to* **page 2.**

**2** But Jake doesn't think so. "I don't know what made the noise, but it wasn't a meteor. They always burn up before they reach the earth. And it certainly wasn't a flying saucer. You don't believe in that nonsense, do you?"

You're not so sure. You'd like to investigate now, but Jake wants to go home.

*If you try to find out now what made the splashing noise, turn to* **page 4.**

*If you decide to wait until morning, turn to* **page 6.**

You decide it's too dangerous to follow the creature. You swim to the edge
of the quarry and take off your mask.

"Oh no!" You see a squirrel digging
in the piles of leaves where you hid
the pods. You leap out of the water
and try to run.

CRASH! You've tripped over your
fins and fallen flat on your face, scaring
the squirrel away. You rip off your fins
and look through the leaves. Thank
goodness the pods are still safe!

You hold onto the pods tightly now
and put on dry clothes. You haven't
been able to find the creature on your
own. Maybe it's time to visit Uncle
Max.

*Turn to* **page 28.**

**4**      You decide to investigate now. Jake waits on top of Death Rock as you take the steep path down to the water. At the edge of the creek you stop and stare. You see the outline of purple stars beneath the water. They sparkle faintly in the darkness. "Jake, you're not going to believe this," you shout. "The water has sparkles in it!"

But Jake won't come down to look. "I don't care if you see a little pink man with two sets of eyes. I'm tired and I want to go home. If you're not up here by the time I count to ten, I'm leaving without you."

You can tell Jake means what he says, so you decide that you'll have to come back tomorrow.

*Turn to* **page 6.**

"HELP!!!" You scream as loud as you can. A moment later, your father rushes in. But when he switches on the light, your room is empty.

"What's all the fuss about?" Jake asks as he stumbles into the room.

You explain what happened, but your brother just laughs. "You're imagining things again," he says. You can tell that he is going to say something about the monster, but you give him a dirty look and he keeps quiet.

"Go back to sleep," says your father. "If anyone was here, we scared him away."

*Turn to* **page 52.**

**6**     The next day, you grab a banana from the refrigerator and head back to the creek. Murphy's Creek is as peaceful as ever. Then you notice strange seed pods floating on the water. They are purple and shaped like stars, with fuzzy red spikes sticking out all around. You kneel down and put a few pods in your pocket. At the same moment a bullfrog spots one of the pods. He flicks out his tongue and gobbles it up.

You can't believe your eyes. The bullfrog shivers violently. Then his skin puffs out like a lumpy balloon. Before you know it, he has turned into a creature about half your size. He has bulging eyes, pointy ears, and a pot belly. The Thing looks around, then waddles out of the creek toward you.

*Turn to* **page 8.**

**8**     You're really scared. You could run home and get Jake so that you don't have to face The Thing alone. But what if the creature is gone by then? You could also stay put and see what happens. After all, The Thing looks pretty weird, but he might not be dangerous.

*If you decide to go get Jake, turn to* **page 11.**

*If you decide to stay and see what happens, turn to* **page 14.**

You take Murf home with you. He follows you inside and sits down at the kitchen table. Your mother is working in her office upstairs. But she might come down any minute. You've got to get Murf down into the basement, and fast. You open the basement door. But Murf won't budge. If you can find something to eat that Murf likes, maybe you can lure him down the stairs.

First you offer him some sardines. He sniffs at them, but won't take a bite. Next you try a chicken leg. But he still won't eat. *Could he be a vegetarian?* you wonder. You offer him some sprouts, but he won't even look at them. You decide to try just one more time. You find an ice-cream pop in the freezer and hand it to Murf.

Hooray! He loves it. But before you can get him into the basement, you hear footsteps in the hall. It's your mother!

*Turn to* **page 10.**

**10**    She takes one look at Murf and turns white as a sheet. She tries to speak, but the words won't come. "Wait a second, Mom . . . I can explain," you say. And you try to tell her the whole story.

Your mother won't listen. She insists on calling the police. She's afraid that Murf might carry a strange virus. Or even radiation.

You don't want the police to take Murf away, but your mother is already on the phone. If you act fast, you and Murf could run away. Or you could wait outside until the authorities arrive. After all, you don't think Murf is dangerous, but you can't really be sure.

*If you decide to wait for the police, turn to* **page 13.**

*If you decide to run away with Murf, turn to* **page 32.**

You run back to the house and try to wake up Jake. "There's a monster in Murphy's Creek!" you shout. But Jake just buries his head under the pillow and groans. Finally you make him come with you back to the creek. But when you get there, The Thing is gone.

Jake is disgusted. He doesn't believe you saw anything special. You show him the pods, but Jake just shrugs. "So what? There are zillions of pods in the woods around here. Look, I'm sorry, kid, but I'm going back to bed."

"But I really saw him!" you protest, as Jake walks away. "If it'll make you feel better," Jake calls over his shoulder, "go show the pods to Uncle Max."

*Turn to* **page 12.**

**12**    Max is a scientist who is interested in all kinds of weird stuff. This should be right up his alley.

You start walking toward Max's house, which is about a mile away. Then you spot a set of tracks in the mud by the edge of the creek. They look like they were made by webbed feet.

*If you decide to follow the tracks, turn to* **page 21.**

*If you decide to show Max the pods, turn to* **page 28.**

From outside, you hear someone talking with your mother. You take Murf's hand and lead him into the kitchen. There's a man there. He's in a white coat.

"I'm Dr. Kramer from the Science Squad," he says, shaking your hand. "We work with the police."

"Hello," you answer. "This is Murf."

"Why don't you tell me the whole story," the doctor says. "I've been talking with your mother, but I'd rather hear it from you."

You take a deep breath and tell him about the meteor shower, and how the next day you found the pods, and how the frog ate one . . . and how it then . . . well, turned into Murf.

"Hmmm. . . ." frowns the doctor, looking Murf up and down. "Before anything else, we have to find all the pods."

*Turn to* **page 31.**

**14**    You decide to stay where you are. A shiver runs up and down your spine as you watch The Thing wade out of the creek. Maybe he'll seem less scary if you give him a name. *Why not Murf?* you ask yourself. After all, he came from Murphy's Creek.

You want to show Murf that you are friendly, but it's hard to know what to do. You look at the banana you are holding in your hand. You've eaten half of it, but decide to offer the rest to the creature. He takes a bite, then spits it out, giving you a dirty look.

*Go on to the next page.*

Even though he didn't like the banana, you realize that Murf may be
hungry. "If you come with me," you
say to him, "I'll find you something
good to eat." You don't think that he
can really understand you, but when
you start walking away, Murf follows.
You reach the shed at the edge of the
field behind your house. Maybe it
would be smarter to leave Murf in the
shed. If you bring him home, you'll
have to hide him in the basement.
Otherwise your mother might get upset. She doesn't even like pets in the
house.

*If you leave Murf in the shed,*
*turn to* **page 23.**

*If you take him home with you,*
*turn to* **page 9.**

**16**     You unstrap your hand, then run to release Murf. But the doctor gets there before you. "Where do you think you're going?" the doctor says in a mean voice, grabbing you roughly by the neck.

Now you're sure that something is really wrong. "I'll bet you're not even a doctor," you say.

"And you'd be right," the doctor grins. Between his lips you see sharp fangs instead of teeth. "Since you're so smart," he continues, "I bet you'd like to know who I am."

With that, he rips off his white coat. Underneath, he isn't a man at all— he's a creature just like Murf, only grown up.

*Turn to* **page 18.**

**18** "I come from the planet Kom, like this young one," the creature explains. "But he is no good to us anymore. For some reason, he seems to like you. He will have to learn that humans are our enemies."

Holding tight to your wrist, the creature unstraps Murf and shoves you both into a secret room. Before he locks the door, he says, "Don't worry, I'll let you out when the time is right." Then he laughs. "But only after the Creatures of Kom have conquered the Earth!"

**THE END**

You ask Murf to wait behind a tree. Then you walk up to a kid who has just struck out. "I'll bet you five dollars I can make you scream."

The older boy looks down at you, "Don't make me laugh," he says. "But I don't mind taking your money."

You lead him over to where Murf is hiding. Murf makes a face and sticks out his tongue. The boy shrieks, then runs to tell his friends. You win the bet!

*Turn to* **page 20.**

**20** Now everybody wants to see Murf. You decide to charge a dollar a look. You lead each kid over to Murf, and he growls and hisses and rolls his eyes. You can tell that Murf loves all the attention. Ten minutes later, you are back on the road with lots of money in your pocket.

You buy ice cream for Murf and two hamburgers for yourself. Then you sit down on a log to eat. This is a pretty good life, you think.

Thanks to Murf, you can earn money wherever you go. You'll travel from town to town, eating and sleeping wherever you like. And if you get tired of your adventure you can always go home—with lots of money in your pocket!

**THE END**

You follow the tracks into the woods. Now and then you catch a glimpse of the creature. But he's moving too fast for you to catch up. After fifteen minutes, you hear a splash up ahead. You run past some bushes into a clearing. In front of you is the quarry where you and Jake like to swim. The creature paddles to the middle, then dives neatly out of sight.

*Turn to* **page 22.**

You stare at the water for five minutes, but the creature doesn't surface. Then you remember that you keep your swimming gear hidden behind a boulder. You make up your mind to dive after the creature. But first you hide the pods under a pile of leaves where they'll be safe.

*Turn to* **page 30.**

You leave Murf in the shed and lock the door. Five minutes later you return with a tray of food. But he is gone. He escaped by digging a tunnel.

You decide to leave the food anyway: a peanut butter sandwich, an apple, and some chocolate-chip ice cream.

Two hours later, the ice cream is gone. You get some more, and leave it for him. It makes you feel good to know that Murf is visiting the shed to look for food.

*Turn to* **page 24.**

**24**     That night a clap of thunder wakes you up from a deep sleep. A terrible storm is raging outside. The window rattles and you get nervous. It might be the wind. Or it might be . . . well, something . . . trying to get in.

The wind howls even louder. You think you hear the window open. You're almost sure that someone—or something—is in the room!

You could scream for help. But you'd feel pretty silly if nothing is there. You could also switch on the light and see for yourself.

*If you scream for help,*
*turn to* **page 5.**

*If you turn on the light,*
*turn to* **page 34.**

You keep walking until you come to the edge of town. You're really starving and the smell of apples makes you look around. Beyond the next field you see an orchard. You think: *No one will mind if we eat a few apples that have fallen on the ground.*

You and Murf climb over a barbed wire fence. Eagerly you bite into a crisp, delicious apple. Murf looks doubtful, but he does the same thing. Before you can take a second bite, you hear a dog barking. The next thing you know, he's crouching a few feet away. His teeth are bared and he's snarling. He looks mean. And a moment later he lunges for you.

*Turn to* **page 26.**

"Quick, Murf! Follow me!" you shout, scrambling up a tree. Just in time, Murf jumps high and grabs hold of a branch. The mad dog is left snapping at his heels.

You're happy that Murf is safe. But now you're worried. What other dangers lie ahead? Can you really take care of Murf on your own?

*Go on to the next page.*

"I guess we'd better go home," you say to Murf. "We've had enough adventure for one day." When the dog finally goes away, you start the long walk home. A few hours later, when you arrive at your house, you see a strange white truck parked in the driveway.

TOP SECRET SCIENCE SQUAD, says a sign on the van.

*Turn to* **page 13.**

You find Max in his lab. From the inside it looks like a giant greenhouse. There's a pond in the middle, where Max breeds frogs and salamanders. All kinds of plants grow around the pond.

You tell him about seeing The Thing from the creek. Then you show him the pods.

Max frowns. You can tell that he is concentrating. "I can think of two experiments. We could feed a pod to a bullfrog and see if it changes into a creature like the one you saw. Or we could plant a pod and watch it grow."

*If you feed the pod to a bullfrog,*
*turn to* **page 36.**

*If you plant a pod,*
*turn to* **page 40.**

You put on your swimsuit, mask, and fins, and dive into the water. You stay near the surface, but you can see the creature below you in the clear water. He's swimming through an opening in the quarry wall. You want to follow him through the hole. After all, you're good at holding your breath, and the hole is only about five feet down. If you don't like what you see, you can always turn around.

*If you decide to follow the creature through the hole, turn to* **page 39.**

*If you decide it might be too dangerous to follow, turn to* **page 3.**

You take the doctor to Murphy's Creek. He gathers up all the pods he can find. "I think we're ready to leave now. Are you absolutely sure there aren't any more pods?"

You remember the pods in your pocket. The doctor seems pretty nice, but you're not exactly sure what will happen to Murf yet. Maybe you should hold on to the pods for a while until you know more.

*If you decide to keep
hiding the pods,
turn to* **page 44.**

*If you give the pods to the doctor,
turn to* **page 47.**

**32**     You decide to run away. While your mother is still on the phone, you grab Murf's hand and slip out.

You walk for hours and finally reach the next town. You and Murf are tired and hungry. You empty your pockets, but you don't have any money for food.

A few minutes later you pass a field where some older kids are playing baseball. You get an idea. You could bet one of the kids that you can make him scream. After all, Murf is really scary-looking—until you get to know him.

*Go on to the next page.*

You're almost sure your plan will work, but you don't know if Murf will like being stared at. You know he is strange-looking. But you don't want to hurt his feelings. Maybe it would be better to keep walking.

*If you decide to make the bet, turn to* **page 19.**

*If you decide to keep walking, turn to* **page 25.**

You switch on the light, and your mouth drops open in surprise. Murf is standing next to your bed, dripping wet. The thunder booms outside and he shivers in fear. You are glad he came to you when he was afraid.

*Go on to the next page.*

You dry Murf off with a big fluffy towel, and let him stay at the foot of your bed. You fall asleep smiling. You and Murf are going to be friends.

In the morning you remember that your friend Mary Ann has invited you to a costume party. You love parties, and you like Mary Ann, even though she is a little nosy. But then you also remember that Jake's swimming club is racing at the quarry today.

You're a pretty good swimmer, and the kids let you race with them even though you are a little younger. Once you almost beat Jake. You'd love to race him again.

*If you decide to go to the costume party,* turn to **page 55.**

*If you decide to enter the race,* turn to **page 48.**

You and Max decide to feed a pod to one of the frogs on the bank of the pond. The frog seems to like the pod. But nothing else happens. The frog is still a frog.

Max turns to you and ruffles your hair. "Don't feel bad," he says. "I'm sure you thought you saw a monster." Then he scatters the pods around for the other frogs to eat. Again, nothing happens. A moment later, the biggest bullfrog jumps into the pond. All the others follow him.

*Go on to the next page.*

As soon as they hit the water, they begin to change. A few seconds later you are staring at a dozen creatures. And the creatures are staring at you.

"Of course!" Max exclaims. "The pod must need water to work. How interesting. Now I can study how the creatures live in a group."

You notice that the biggest creature is making signs to the others. Then all of them start moving towards you very slowly. "Are you sure they're . . . well, friendly?" you ask Max.

*Turn to* **page 38.**

Max doesn't have a chance to answer. Suddenly the creatures rush forward and jump on you and your uncle. One creature stuffs a pod in your mouth and another forces you to swallow. After they do the same thing to Max, they shove you both into the pond.

"NO! NO!" you shout. But you feel your body changing. You look at Max and start to scream. Then you see your own reflection in the water. You've turned into a creature just like him!

Would you believe this is really . . .

**THE END**

You take a deep breath and follow the creature through the hole. At first you can't see anything in the greenish gloom. Then you spot the creature. But he isn't alone. There are four others just like him!

As soon as you appear, they swim around in a circle. They seem glad to see you. But you need a breath of air. Now they're whirling faster and faster around you. They've created a whirl-pool that you can't swim through!

Maybe swimming after the creature wasn't such a great idea. Better luck next time! Glug . . . glug . . . glug. . . .

## THE END

**40**     You and Max decide to plant a pod. You pick a spot where the earth is damp, right in front of a rose bush. Max waters the pod carefully. "If we're lucky," he says, "in a week it will begin to sprout."

You walk to the greenhouse door. When you get there, the ground in front of the rose bush splits open and a plant shoots out of the earth. It looks like a giant asparagus, except that it has a huge rose on top.

Max rushes over to examine the plant. "Be careful!" you shout. But it's too late. As Max gets close, the plant leans over. You see two rows of big, jagged teeth in the middle of the rose. The next thing you know, the plant picks up Max and swallows him!

*Go on to the next page.*

"EEEEEEEEEEK!" You close your
eyes and scream when you see the rose
stretch out and bend towards you.
You're so scared that you can't even
move. . . .

**41**

*Turn to* **page 42.**

**42**    "Don't eat me! Don't eat me!" you shout. But when you open your eyes, the rose is gone. You're not even in Uncle Max's greenhouse. You're lying on the bank of Murphy's Creek, safe and sound.

What's going on? Could you have fallen asleep the morning after the meteor shower and dreamt the whole thing? You look around again. There are no creatures. Or giant roses. Or anything special at all.

*Go on to the next page.*

By now the dream has faded. You stand up and start for home. On the way you see a strange, star-shaped pod. Without thinking, you put it in your pocket. *One of these days, I'm going to have a real adventure*, you say to yourself. *And I have a funny feeling that it's going to be soon!*

## THE END

**44**     You feel the pods in your pocket, but you don't say anything. "All right, then," says Doctor Kramer. "I'll be taking Murf off to the research center now."

As you walk back to the van, you ask if you can come, too. But the doctor says no. All the work at the research center is top secret. No visitors are allowed.

You are surprised when Dr. Kramer pushes Murf into the van. "Wait a second!" you shout. But the doctor doesn't seem to hear you. He starts the van and drives away.

*Go on to the next page.*

Murf's gone and you miss him. There is nothing you can do to get him back. Or is there? If your idea works, you may soon have another playmate just like him.

Before you can change your mind, you run back to Murphy's Creek and place a pod on a lily pad. Then you watch a bullfrog hop over and flick out his tongue. . . .

**THE END**

You reach into your pocket and pull out a fistful of pods. "Here are some more," you say to the doctor. After he wraps them carefully in a plastic bag, the doctor drives you and Murf to the hospital.

"We have to run tests to see if you've been hurt by the pods," the doctor explains as you enter the building.

The doctor straps you into a chair, then hooks you up to a dozen machines. Then he does the same thing to Murf. You notice that he forgot to strap down one of your arms, but you decide not to say anything.

*If you try to escape,
turn to* **page 16.**

*If you stay put and
hope for the best,
turn to* **page 50.**

**48**     You decide to stay home and enter the race. You leave Murf in your room when it's time to meet Jake. You lock the door, but the window lock is broken. You just hope he doesn't decide to follow you.

At the quarry, Jake is joking around with his friends. "Where's your monster now, kiddo?" he teases when he sees you.

You're mad at your brother for teasing you in front of his friends. But you decide not to say anything about Murf. Jake wouldn't believe you anyway.

*Go on to the next page.*

The team decides that you will swim in five races. You win two and you lose two. Finally, it's your turn to swim against Jake.

"Ready! Set! Go!" shouts the captain. As you dive into the water, you think you see Murf at the far end of the quarry. But your mind is on the race and you can't be sure.

Now you're swimming as fast as you can. But halfway across you are two lengths behind. Then suddenly you feel yourself going faster. Something cold and slimy is pushing you along. Could it be Murf?

*Turn to* **page 58.**

**50** You stay where you are. Dr. Kramer turns on the machines, which beep and buzz and whirr. Then he pokes and prods you with his hands. "You are in perfect health," he says when he finishes.

"That's good," you say, "but what will happen to Murf?"

"Don't worry," says the doctor. "I'm sure he'll be happy here." He draws back a curtain and you see that one wall of the room is made of glass. On the other side you see a dozen creatures just like Murf. Then the doctor opens a door and Murf rushes to join his friends.

*Go on to the next page.*

"We think the creatures are from another planet," the doctor explains, "and we hope you will help us study them. You see, you're the only human who has been able to make friends."

You agree to help, and the doctor shakes your hand. "Come back the day after tomorrow," he says, handing you a special badge. "Show this to the guard and he'll let you in."

You look at the badge and grin. It's hard to believe that you're really a Junior Member of the Secret Science Squad. You can't wait to see what will happen next.

**THE END**

**52**    The next day, you visit the shed to look for Murf. Yesterday's ice cream has melted. For the rest of the week, you leave more ice cream every day. But Murf doesn't come back to eat it.

By the end of the week, you're beginning to think that Jake is right — you've been imagining things.

On Saturday you go to a picnic with your brother and his friends. They are a year older than you, but they let you tag along. After you eat, Jake says, "Let's go on a scavenger hunt. Whoever finds the most interesting thing wins the game."

*Go on to the next page.*

All the kids scatter in the woods. You find an old yo-yo under a tree and start back to the clearing. On the way, you hear some leaves rustle. You spin around and see Murf sitting on a rock. He seems glad to see you and takes your hand. Together you march back to the picnic area. You can't wait to see Jake's face when he sees Murf.

Your brother found an old arrowhead and his friend Ziggy found a rusty fishing rod.

But nobody found anything quite like Murf.

## THE END

You decide to take Murf to the costume party. You'll tell your friends that he's your cousin.

You arrive at the party a little late. When you and Murf enter the room, the contest for best costume has already begun.

You and Murf line up with the others in the front of the room. You're dressed as a ghost, and Mary Ann is dressed as a princess. Some of the others have pretty good costumes. But they decide that Murf's is the best.

*Turn to* **page 56.**

**56**     After Murf wins the prize, it's time to eat ice cream and cake. The other kids take off their masks.

"Aren't you taking your mask off?" Mary Ann asks Murf. "Come on, I want to try it on."

"Leave Murf alone," you say. "He's really shy."

But nosy Mary Ann won't listen. She jumps forward and grabs Murf's face. Murf makes a weird noise like a tug-boat.

*Go on to the next page.*

Mary Ann squeals and jumps away. "IT'S ALL SLIMY!!" she shrieks. "HE'S REAL! HE'S REAL!" Now everyone screams and runs from the room.

You and Murf are all alone with the ice cream and cake. You're a little upset. "Well, Murf, it looks like the party is over," you say to him. But Murf doesn't mind. He's busy eating the ice cream all by himself!

## THE END

**58**    You reach the finish line just ahead of your brother. Jake looks stunned. "How did you do it?" he asks.

You start to explain that you think Murf helped you. Then you change your mind. "I've been practicing a lot lately," you say.

Jake slaps you on the back and the other kids cheer.

Out of the corner of your eye, you see Murf stick his head above the water. Then he winks at you and disappears.

**THE END**